T0064459

FIRO RAIDEN

SAMEER HIREMATH

PARTRIDGE
A Penguin Random House Company

Library of Congress Control Number:		2015950356
ISBN:	Softcover	978-1-4828-5301-8
	eBook	978-1-4828-5302-5

To order additional copies of this book, contact
Toll Free 800 101 2657 (Singapore)
Toll Free 1 800 81 7340 (Malaysia)
orders.singapore@partridgepublishing.com

www.partridgepublishing.com/singapore

To my parents, for their love and support

Acknowledgement

Professional publishers offer the unpublished writer a chance to step into the light. Mr. Kinnari, my previous local publisher, loves bringing books to life. Without him, Firo Raiden would be another mass of bits encoded on a hard drive. I'm not sure how you thank someone for making a dream come true. For me, writing a first novel was a harrowing experience. But I imagined that a book was a three-dimensional puzzle, and you just had to rearrange the pieces together. I saw this books as a challenging project, and it definitely proved to be one! This book is just the beginning of a series of projects I intend to get started on as soon as possible. Right then, onward to the thanks:

At home: Both my mom and dad for their constant support, for their advice and for taking a chance on Firo Raiden. My friends, without whom this book wouldn't have been possible.

At School: my teachers, for guiding me, and helping me hone my skills.

At publishers: For their great help and support and for their immense patience. A special thanks to Amit and Sydney, my two editors, for their expertise in punctuation and words small and hippopotomonstrosesquipedalian, abstruse and coined. Ms. Sydney, as I mentioned earlier, for her amazing creativity on the attractive cover page.

And of course, my dear reader. I couldn't have done it without you.

I have said what is needed to be said. The rest is silence.

I hope the stars shine brightly over you.

Sameer Hiremath

Contents

Firo finds himself in a North American forest, armed with a katana, and a bag full of dangerous weapons. Night-eye, a jaguar, joins him on his journey. He meets Mark, Scar and Scotty on the way.

Firo wakes up in a ship, without his weapons or his memory. He befriends Griffin, and with his help, tries to get off the ship. He also searches the ship for Mark, Scar and Scotty, leading him to an unimaginably terrifying monster.

Firo wakes up in a ship, without his weapons or his memory. He befriends Griffin, and with his help, tries to get off the ship. He also searches the ship for Mark, Scar and Scotty, leading him to an unimaginably terrifying monster.

Firo escapes the ship, only to find himself trapped again. Only this time, in Australia. He is determined to uncover his past.

Chapter 1

THE FOREST

Night had just fallen, yet the howls were getting closer and closer. My feet were close to numb, I could barely feel them. I lost my map a few miles back, so now I was completely lost. I just jumped over a small pond, when I realized something was amiss. There was absolutely no noise, which was not possible in a forest. Especially one in North America. I stopped short of a thick bush, straining my ears to catch the slightest noise. There was some rustling, I tensed, and a rabbit hopped out of the bush. "Whoa there little fella!" I said "You scared me half to death!" But my relief was short lived; I was distracted by the rabbit, so I didn't hear the soft padded footsteps behind me. If it wasn't for my training, I would've been sliced right there and then. Some instinct of mine told me of the impending danger, So I slid out my katana; 15" of pure black graphene - 200 times stronger than steel, crafted to perfection; and then, faster than the eye could follow, I whirled around and slashed! My blade found flesh and sliced into it like a hot knife slices through butter. The creature I skewered let out an ear splitting howl, probably to alert the others, just before I slit its throat.

From where I was standing, I could hear them loping through the forest. I quickly took out my iPhone and took a few pictures of the motionless body in front of me, and quietly melded into the shadows of the trees, invisible to everything and everyone but myself. Just in time too, as the first of the creatures jumped into the clearing where the creature I killed lay. One of them, it seemed to me to be the leader, sniffed around the body and motioned towards the others. Two of them came into the clearing, and one lifted the body on top of the other and set off at a fast pace through the forest, towards the denser areas. As I took in more and more of the scene in front of me, I noticed that there were hundreds of them! Seems like they're pretty desperate to capture me! I chuckled, catching myself halfway. Too late! One of them turned towards me, sniffed for a bit, and then let out a low growl, alerting all the others, including the leader. Without warning, they broke into a run towards me! Luckily, I was a fast runner, Junior Cross Country good! I took off in god knows what direction. Just wanting to get away from there, with the pack in pursuit. Adrenaline was pumping through my body, causing my senses to go hyper. My mind was on overdrive, automatically dodging and weaving through trees. But no matter how fast I ran, they were always a few meters behind me.

I could feel their breath on the back of my neck. I couldn't go on like this forever, so I started formulating a plan. Then like lightning, it hit me! I got it! I put on more speed, and then veered off course, taking my pursuers by surprise. I took out my hand grenade; I was tiring quickly, so I had to work fast. I took a length of coiled wire from my backpack, and looped it around the grenade's pin, with the other end of the wire in my hand. I tossed it into the midst of my pursuers. Seems like they have a lot of safety learning to do, because at once, all of them converged on it. I made a mental countdown, 'Three, two, one-'I pulled the wire, waiting for the explosion to happen. But nothing, then suddenly, there was a flash of light, then- KABLAAAM! The Einsteins behind me flew apart. Literally. Each of them flew backwards; arms and legs were ripped loose by the magnitude of my grenade. All of their blood and guts rained over the treetops, as if the devil himself was having a gore party. I stopped and looked behind me, and saw entrails, pieces of limbs and other body parts that I can't mention in this book. Oh wait, have I even introduced myself? Silly me! Taking you on a ride like that when you don't even know me!

Well, I'm Firo Raiden of the Kamikaze clan in a remote part of east Japan. Ha! I'm just messing with you. I'm from California, actually. Yeah, it probably sounds like I'm an average guy and everything, you've got that right. I'm an orphan. My parents were murdered in their sleep. They worked for a secret organization called *Hatboro Netsuke*, a Ninja Assassin camp. They were assassinated.

Ironic, no? Ninja Assassins, assassinated by other Ninja Assassins. One good thing, I seemed to inherit the dexterity and skill of a Ninja. I guess my Parents were tall, because I was 5'7" at the age of eleven. Now, I'm about 6'1". I was a little on the slim side, but what I lost in muscle, I seemed to have made up in Brains. I was just 3 years old when I was whisked away to a quiet little orphanage in North America. Canada, to be exact. I was treated like filth over there, somehow surviving for 11 years. I was also strangely good at any and every sport that the orphanage offered. You name it; I'm the best at it. Football, basketball, tennis, volleyball, to name a few. I had the uncanny knack of balance. Everyone over there called me Mr. Assassin, Because of my ability to free run. It was when I was 14; a bunch of crazed scientists came over to 'examine' us kids. I along with a few others, I don't recall their names, were selected for something. I followed along, oblivious to the clearly marked danger. It was after we were locked in with the scientists when I realized that something was amiss. I was on the edge of paranoia, when my fears were confirmed. They brought in a few cages to the room. But get this, these cages were humongous! I looked around, desperately hoping for an idea, but no avail. We were trapped! We screamed and screamed, but it was all in vain. The scientists exited the room, and there was a rumbling noise. I recognized those sounds to be the cage doors opening. There wasn't an escape route. The only way out was through the metal door and that was locked. Panic settled in, some were crying, and some were praying. Then, the cages opened up to reveal some of the most hideous creatures you could ever imagine. I won't go through the details, sadly, as their description cannot be explained by mere words. The next few minutes were absolute chaos. I remember a body flying towards me. But that was the extent of my memory that night. I woke up in the middle of a forest, a katana at my side, an iPhone in my hands, and a backpack full of weapons. I assumed that everyone else in the room with me that night was violently slaughtered.

Ever since then I was on the run from those…those things. But recently, some other animals, I think what they are; have joined in on the chase. I had assumed that everyone else in that room was violently slaughtered. So, for the past month, I was on the run. I averted my eyes from the horrendous scene. I managed to crawl up to a tree, my legs felt like they were going to fall of any moment. I took out my iPhone, to study the picture. I was a little shocked with what I saw. It seemed that some crazy genius merged a tiger with a bear. The claws were way sharper that those of a tiger, and it was shaggier that a bear. Its fur was darker than coal. My iPhone started beeping. 'Damn!' I thought, 'Battery's dead!' I tucked it back into my pocket. I looked around, surprised that it was dark already. I realized with a start that it was way past 10 p.m. I needed to find shelter, and fast! Unless I wanted to become a walking buffet. I looked around for some firewood, and found some at the base of a tree, probably left behind by someone, and set to make a fire. I rummaged through the backpack. Score! A mini flamethrower! It took me a few seconds to understand the mechanism, but I did, and got a good flame going.

I found a commando knife in one of the pockets, and absentmindedly started sharpening it. It wasn't long before sleep had found me, and dragged me into its dark realm. I slept long and deep, the best kind of sleep I've had in ages! Lucky for me, there weren't any dreams plaguing me. I awoke to the sound of a robin chirping, the sunlight beating down on my bare skin, wishing that everyday could be like today. I rubbed the sleep from my eyes, yawning while I was at it. I stretched for a while, doing some pushups just for the heck of it. I did some meditation, the fresh air filling my lungs.

Then the chirping stopped, there was a fluttering sound, telling me that the robin had flown away. I stood up straight, ready for action. I heard the unmistakable sound of twigs snapping. I slowly took out my knife, leaving my katana at my side. As I gripped the knife, I caught a glimpse of something black. I shivered a bit, thinking of the creature I killed. "Time to man up, Firo" I thought to myself, just as the animal came into my peripheral vision. I was both surprised and relieved to see a jaguar. A cub, to be exact. I've never actually seen a jaguar cub up close and personal, and I've got to admit, looking at its sleek and glossy body and those rippling muscles, it seemed like Mother Nature had outdone herself again. The jaguar came closer and closer.

I stood still, unsure of what to do. I felt my pockets, finding some leftover turkey jerky. I tossed it towards the jaguar, and it swallowed the jerky in one bite! I looked around for signs of any other food, but no avail. The jaguar inched closer and closer, yet I made no move. Suddenly, it pounced on me! I thought it was going to rip out my throat, that I was a goner. But it did something even more surprising, it LICKED me! Can you believe it? "Whoa there girl, down, down!" I said half-choking. I think she understood me, because she got off me, and patiently sat in front of me. I got up, wiping the drool off my face, and stared at the jaguar. A jaguar. A LIVE jaguar. I didn't know what to do. Take her with me? She seemed like she could manage, like me; she probably was a runaway. But the responsibility of watching over her was big.

I was still pondering over this, when she spoke! Well, not with words, but sort of telepathically. I heard her in my mind. She said < Thank you for the meat.> She caught me off guard. I yelped, and jumped back. <Do not worry, Oh kind one.> 'Oh what the heck', I thought. "Is there any way I could communicate like this?" I asked. <Yes, but first, we must join minds.> "And how do I do that?" <Imagine me in your mind, picture me joint to you.>

"Like a rope attached from me to you?" <Rope? What is that?> "Nothing." I said. I proceeded to do what she said. And suddenly, I was aware of another presence along with mine. It seemed vast and alien compared to mine. Then suddenly, I felt some sort of connection between us. I thought of releasing my mind from hers, but she said <Do not be afraid, just h o l d o n u n t i l I t e l l y o u t o r e l e a s e . > I felt tingly all over, especially on the back of my neck. After a few minutes of silence, she told me to release my hold on her. I did just that, and suddenly, I felt like my arm was missing. I guessed that she felt the same way. <We have bonded, Oh kind one!> "Call me Firo" I said. <My name is Night-eyes> said she. I sat down, dazed, and she came over to snuggle with me. I was stroking her hair, when I heard the noise. I silently stood up, with night-eyes ready by my side. That's when I saw a flash of white and realized that we had unwanted visitors. I tried the thought speak, and I found that it was much easier now that we were bonded. <Night-eyes, we have enemies.> she just growled, a low throaty one, and somehow I knew that she was warning the creatures to back off. But it was of no use, as they came out of the underbrush, facing us. I counted 10, but I couldn't be sure.

It seemed that they were newer versions of the others I faced yesterday. They were bigger; their snouts were more elongated, and their mouths were gapped, so you could see their razor sharp teeth. Their claws were blood red, but the rest of their body was covered in white fur. That seemed odd, but I had no time to think, because at once they leaped towards us. Even before I could slide out my katana, I saw a black shadow fly past me. Night- eyes! I chuckled to myself, and readied myself on the balls of my feet, with my katana in my hands. Three of the beasts made the mistake of coming too close. With a lightning fast strike, I left two beheaded, and sliced off the limbs of the third. I looked around for Night-eyes, and found her battling another creature fiercely, with blood in her mouth, and rage burning in her eyes; I wouldn't fancy my chances against her in battle! I saw a lot of bodies around her, throats bitten off. 'That's one hell of a jaguar!' I thought. I turned around only to find another creature circling me. This one seemed to be the leader, because it was HUGE! It probably could make Bigfoot run home screaming!

I ran towards it, dodging the rocks it threw at me with ease, and I jumped straight at it, about 4 meters high. A new record! I landed on its back and thrust my sword into its spine.

Good news? Nothing. Bad news? I think it got a 'little' pissed that a kid was poking a stick into its back. It shook its body violently; I was thrown off it back, and crashed into a tree. I tried to stand up, but I fell back down. The creature was only a few meters away, looking for me. I looked to my right and saw Night-eyes crushing her opponent. She jumped onto its back, and started chewing at its throat. There was blood flying everywhere, like a sprinkler. The creature fell down with a heavy thud and an audible 'crack' told me that it had crushed its skull. I looked back around, and saw that the leader lumbering towards me. Suddenly, a black ball of fury hurtled past me. Night-eyes pounced onto the creatures face, aiming at its eyes. The creature shook its head, trying to get her off, but Night-eyes held on. She managed to claw at its eyes, taking one out with a sickening 'POP'.

The creature howled in pain, and tried to reach Night-eyes, who was too agile to be caught. She tried to get the other eye, but she lost her footing, and crashed to the ground painfully.

The beast was about to pick her up in its jaws, when I shouted, "Hey ugly! Yeah you! Your mama's a gorilla!" Well, it left Night-eyes alone, and came towards me. I slipped my knife into my hands, and lobbed it with all my strength towards the creature's eye. It struck true to its target! The creature howled for the last time, and crashed to the ground, with an earth shattering 'BOOM!'

Night-eyes limped towards me, whimpering with pain. "Hey there girl, let me look at that wound." She whined, and shook her head furiously." It's okay, I'll be very careful" slowly, I extended my arm into my backpack, took out some gauze wrap, and gently took her hind leg. It looked really messy; there was a deep red gash all the way from her hip to her paw. I looked around and saw that we somehow landed in a balsam poplar groove. I racked up my general knowledge, and remembered- The balsam poplar bears buds coated with a gooey, fragrant substance. Applied externally, it helps heal wounds. A friend had once used this on me, after I had cut my elbow on a branch. I took out one of the buds, and smeared it Night-eyes' wound. The effect was instantaneous!

One minute there was a large gaping gash, the next minute; it was just a tiny scar! Night-eyes had fallen unconscious, so I had to lift her up. I walked a few miles without breaking a sweat, but I had to stop for Night-eyes' sake. I managed to make some sort of primitive shelter out of leaves, twigs and rocks. It wasn't exactly the Burj Al-Khalifa, but it would suffice. I laid her down on a bed of flowers, obscured from the world. I must say, I've outdone myself yet again! The camouflage cover kept us warm and hidden at the same time. I crept in next to Night-eyes, to keep her warm. I covered up the entrance, and lay down. I was lost in my thoughts, when, all of a sudden, there was a ripping sound, followed by a squeal of pain. I heard the distinct sounds of voices in the clearing, and peeped through a hole I made in the covering. What I saw was strange. Three men, no…'men' isn't the right word, more like three Godzilla offspring, why? Because they were at least 7 feet tall! And they had muscles that would have looked proper on a silverback gorilla! They were talking amongst themselves just a few meters away from my shelter. They were speaking in another language, Russian I think, I could make out some of the words, though. I caught words like; 'jaguar' and 'boy'. I understood that they were hunting me, and they planned to capture me, alive or dead.

I felt something on my shoulder, and I turned around finding Night-eyes standing up straight. <Are you ok now?> I asked. <Yes Firo, my leg is much better now. Thank you.> < Don't mention It.> I turned back around to look through the hole. The scene had completely changed! One moment, there were three men professionally revising their plans, and the next moment, there was utter confusion. I counted two men, out of the three. Both of them seemed scared and shocked. I didn't know what was wrong, until I saw the blood on the trees. Something must have happened to one of them. I focused on my surroundings, noting anything that seemed out of the ordinary. When I saw a few bits of metal in the trees closest to me. It seemed that something had exploded. 'My shelter must have protected me and Night-Eyes!' I thought. I noticed movement behind the men, just out of their sight. It looked like a man, but with the things that had happened to me the past few days; I'd have been surprised if it was a human. As it moved closer and closer to the men, still keeping out of sight, I caught a proper look at it. I wasn't human (no surprise there.), but nor was it an animal. It had a face that was horribly disfigured, like a three-year old was let loose with a jar of putty.

Its body wasn't proportionate, like an upside down snowman. Its legs were really long; it looked a bit like my dorm warden on a bad hair day! I figured that it would make short work of them, when I saw something that made my heart stop. I hadn't noticed it before; I was too preoccupied with the danger of the men spotting my hideout that I didn't notice it at all. Before I could make any move, there was a ripping sound. I looked up to find my makeshift roof in shreds. A face peeped down towards me and Night-eyes. I was about to dice him up with my blade, but he motioned for me to keep quiet. I was a little surprised, but I decided to play along. For now. I jumped out, making sure that the others in the clearing couldn't see me. Night-eyes followed me out, <I sense friendliness, Firo. I think we should listen to him.> she said. <If it's okay with you, it's okay with me> I replied. I turned around to the stranger. Now that I was much closer, and had a better view of him, he seemed young, maybe a year or two younger than me, with a face that showed signs of bad acne. He was dressed in camouflage, with a sniper rifle hanging loose from his back. "What's your name, kid?" I asked. "It's Scott. Scott Johansson. You can call me Scotty. That's what everyone back at camp calls me."

He said. He had a thick accent, a bit of Russian with American. That created a guttural voice, just an octave lower than mine. "My name's Firo. This is Night-eyes." <Pleased to meet you, Scotty.> Night- Eyes said. If he was surprised, he sure hid it well. His face remained expressionless as he said, "Pleasure's entire mine, miss" his face splitting with a grin. Then he whistled softly. There was a rustling in the bushes, and two other boys came into view. They looked like they might've been twins, thick black hair, stubby noses, big ears, you know, the works. They were bulky; it looked like they could bench press 250 pounds. And that was with one hand! They looked almost comical, I thought, when I saw a flash of jealousy cross Scotty's face, but I must've been imagining it. He was a matchstick compared to the two hulks. "My name is Mark, and this is Scar." Said one of them. I couldn't differentiate between them,-So I asked "How do I know who is who?" One of them gave me a grin saying "I'm mark, and, uh, Scar's the one with the scar." He gave me a look that said "I have the IQ of a fencepost."

I looked closer and saw a thin line running from his eyebrow down to his jaw. Mark piped up, saying, "You aren't the only ones who can communicate, you know." "What do you mean?" I asked. Mark whistled, a low whistle, and a red tail hawk flew out from one of the trees, and landed on his arm. "This is Wind-Breaker." He said, with a hint of pride. <Good to meet you, Firo and you, Night-eyes.> I wasn't surprised that she knew our names, red tails have e x c e l l e n t h e a r i n g . < S a m e h e r e, W i n d - Breaker.>suddenly, there was a scream from behind us. I had forgotten all about the three men in the clearing! "Oh @#$%!" Scotty shouted." What the hell was that?! "Wind-Breaker took off, and was back a few moments later, probably scouting report. She thought spoke with Mark. Mark's face blanched in a n i n s t a n t, n o d o u b t w i t h b a d n e w s . He let Wind-Breaker fly, probably having a plan of their own. Scotty hefted his rifle, looking nervous. I realized that it must've been his first time in an actual fight. They took off towards the clearing, dodging and weaving through the trees. Scotty looked at me, and said "What the hell is happening?" I shushed him with a wave of my hand, and slid out my katana. He looked at the blade in awe.

"Listen, I'm pretty sure that there's something dangerous out there. I need you to follow me." I said. He nodded in understanding. I crept towards the clearing, fearing the worst, when Night-eyes nipped my leg lightly. <Firo, I fear the worst. Be careful.> <Of course, Night-eyes.> Man, I've got this thought speaking thing in the bag! I took out my flamethrower, a small compact thing, and held it tightly in my hand, with my katana in the other. I set the tip of my blade on fire, making it white hot. As I stowed the flamethrower back into my backpack, I pushed aside some leaves, and observed the scene. It was utter chaos. There wasn't a living soul there. There was enough blood to open a chain of blood banks! Bits and pieces of guts were scattered across the muddy ground. I think I saw an eyeball up in the trees. There was some movement just in the corner of my vision. I looked to find that Mark and Scotty had circled the field. Their faces were covered in disgust. Night-eyes and windbreaker were already checking some of the corpses scattered here and there. <Firo! Duck!> the only thing that saved me was the urgency in Night-eyes' voice. I did so without hesitation, just as a scythe passed above my head, grazing my hair, and burying itself into a tree.

Scotty fired a shot in the direction the scythe flew in and a shout told us that he got a bulls-eye. Mark looked at Windbreaker and I knew that he just thought-spoke with her. She flew up, lost in the harsh sunlight for a few seconds, and dived at the attacker out of nowhere with a ferocious screech. But a dagger intercepted her; she crashed to the ground with a sickening crunch. "NO!" the one syllable echoed across the clearing, as Mark leapt to the fallen bird. I turned around, and saw a figure covered in robes. There was a hood covering his face, preventing others from looking at him, there was a whistling sound, and by instinct, I jerked my head back just as a shruiken passed by my face. 'Damn!' I thought. He was fast! I barely saw his hands move. But before he could make another move, there was a yell from behind me. And a second later there was another shot, embedding itself in the attacker's forearm. He barely glanced at his wound. I realized that we had a real enemy on our hands; the beast I saw before was just a distraction! I noticed his hands move, and dived for cover, taking Scar down with me. There was a horrible shriek behind me; I risked a glance just to see Night-eyes! She somehow managed to get behind the robed creature, and now she was hanging off its back, chewing at its skull.

There was a foul stench in the air; I guessed that it was coming from the creature. I stood up, helping Scar as I did. I looked for Mark, and found him kneeling over the limp bird. There were tears falling from his face onto the frail, body. I hurried to his side, "It's going to be okay, Mark. We'll fix her up, but now, we really need to get the hell outta here!" I said. He said something unintelligible and continued rocking in silence. Scotty came over to me, "What the heck is that thing!?" I ignored him; there would be time to answer him later. I helped Mark up on his feet, a record if I have to say! Scar came over to help. I told him about what I saw back there, and about the plan I made. He understood, and set off. If you're wondering what it was, then I'll tell you. I saw a body tied to a post, it looked like a girl, but I couldn't be sure. I knew that I had to save her, no matter what. Fancy that! Little old 'Raiden playing hero! I told Scar to cut her free from the rope that she was tied with. I turned around, and saw that Night-eyes was losing her battle. She wouldn't last long by herself. "Hey!" I shouted, doubting my insanity at the same time. I wouldn't last long in battle with this THING. I steadied myself on the balls of my feet, as I did so many times before, on the jungle-gym.

I had just grasped my center of gravity, when Night- Eyes was thrown off due to sheer force of the creature. I knew she'd be okay, so it didn't matter. The beast bellowed a challenge towards me. I would have crapped my pants there and then, but lucky me. I hadn't eaten anything for the past two days. I gripped my katana so hard, my knuckles were turning white. I waited for it to make its first move. It hefted another scythe off its back. Great. Just great. I could only hope that Scar would save her/him before I died. Well, that was my plan. It lifted it up to its thigh, readying itself. I hesitantly stepped forward, trying to (unsuccessfully) cover up my fear. The creature cocked it head to its side, confused. I didn't know what was happening, until I looked at my katana. The diamond set in the center was glowing. Not because of the sun or anything, but literally, GLOWING. That was odd, it never did that before. There was a tickling sensation all across my arm, from my palm. I suddenly felt stronger, my stomach stopped rumbling for food, and I felt all hopped up, like I was a squirrel on caffeine. I looked at my foe with renewed strength, I could sense hesitation in the attacker, and I leapt up into the air, directly over my attacker, and brought my katana down in an arc.

I was aiming for its head, but it dodged, and I cut off its arm. The creature screamed at me in pain. Now that I was closer, I noticed that it was human-like. It had the same physique. "Who are you?" I demanded. "I'm Dave!" it screamed, writhing in agony on the ground. I was definitely surprised to hear a creature like this, have a name like Dave! I heard a small gasp from behind me; I turned to find Mark and Scotty staring at me. I didn't know why, until I looked down at my skin. It was glowing, and not like those fake skincare products they claim that makes your skin 'glow'. It looked just like the diamond. The diamond in the katana had stopped shining. I yelped, and fell down, rolling in the mud, trying to extinguish myself. I realized that I didn't feel different, so I slowly stood up. I looked back down at Dave, readying myself for whatever gruesome methods I'd probably use to get information from it. Just then, Scar barreled past me, appearing from the bushes with a body bag over his shoulder, stopping short of Mark. "What? What is it?" I asked, already afraid of what the answer might be. "There's something big chasing me," He panted. I didn't see it back there, but lucky me, because it saw me".

I heard heavy padded footsteps behind me. I turned around, ready for anything. Night-Eyes stood beside me. Just as the creature entered the clearing, I felt a sharp jab on my shoulder. I felt around for a while, before realizing that it was an arrow! The blurred vision told me it was a poison. Oh great. This just keeps getting better and better. Before I knew it, I was falling. The last thing I saw was Mark and Scar running away with Scotty providing cover fire. The ground embraced me, and I blacked out.

Chapter 2

STRANDED

I woke to the sound of a scream. My eyes flared open on instinct. I lay on a table, an uncomfortable one, at that. I tried getting up, but I found my arms and legs chained to a table on which I lay on. A sense of dread and panic filled me up. I looked around, taking in my surroundings. I was in some sort of room, a lab. There was a table in the far corner of the room. I could make out a lot of instruments, SHARP instruments. There were footsteps behind me. I tried twisting around to see who it was, but my restraints prevented me from doing so. There was an inaudible murmur, and there was another set of footsteps, this time a quicker pair. I saw a man in a white-coat cross the room, towards the table. The man picked up an especially sharp scalpel, and proceeded to another corner, where there was another table. I was so focused on what the man was doing; I didn't notice the other scientist besides me. I turned my head, and almost jumped out of my skin. He was scribbling something on an official looking clipboard. There was a soft cough to my side. I turned my head, to that direction, and found another white-coat observing me. He was wearing these huge wire-rimmed glasses, maybe the size of my palm.

He was frail; his body was twitching at regular intervals, like he was hopped up on caffeine. He was furiously scribbling something on a notepad that he was carrying. I was staring at him, when suddenly the other man was at my side. Before I could open my mouth to protest, he thrust an oxygen mask over my mouth. I choked, unable to breathe, when he released the oxygen valve, and glorious, glorious oxygen poured into the mask. I inhaled deeply, savoring the cool feeling. I felt a little drowsy at first, but I dismissed it. There was a much stronger wave, and it was then I realized it wasn't an oxygen mask, it was an anesthetic mask! I thrashed around wildly, somehow freeing myself from the shackles. I felt my fist connect with soft flesh. I ripped off the remaining shackles and the mask, and turned to face the other man. He backed up to the table, and grabbed a knife. - "Oh no you don't!" I snarled, as I heaved up the heavy anesthetic cylinder. He looked at me with wild eyes, I didn't have time to stop and pity. I threw the cylinder with an almighty roar. I turned around, not waiting to see where it landed. I heard a crash, a scream and a cracking sound. Then everything was quiet. I headed towards the door, thinking of what to do next, when there was an ear- piercing howl right below me.

I jumped back, startled, when I realized it came from the room below me. I heard another scream, from the room beside mine. I decided to investigate. I proceeded outside cautiously, mind alert. The door to the next room was right in front of to the next room right in front of me. Suddenly, there was a crash, followed by a thud, just behind the door. I barged open into the room, and saw two scientists lying out cold on the floor. There was another man in the room; he didn't see me, his back was turned towards me. He was built like Mark, about 6'5". With a pang of guilt, I realized I had totally forgotten about Mark, Scar and Scotty. No time to worry about them now, I thought. I tip-toed towards the big man. I was just behind him, when I heard him speak, "Come any closer, and I'll kill you." I froze. He slowly turned around, and when he saw me, he exclaimed "But you're only a kid!" "So I've noticed" I said drily. He started to chuckle, but stopped suddenly. There was a scuffle behind the door, and before I made any move, he pulled out a *shruiken* and threw it towards the door. It cut through the wall. "How-"I began, but I was interrupted by a soft shriek from the other side of the wall". A scientist staggered through the doorway, clutching his chest. There was a gaping wound where his lung would've been, I suppose. There was blood all over him. Surprising, how much blood a man can lose in a few seconds with a big enough wound. The blood was flowing like Niagara Falls! He gasped for breath, and slowly sank to his knees and died. I turned around to the man. "Who are y-you?" I stammered. He looked at me skeptically, and finally said, "The name's Griffin". I waited for a last name, and when he didn't give one, I asked, "Griffin what?" "Just call me Griffin". He headed towards the door, and I stopped him, a little nervously. "What is this place?" I asked. "You mean you don't know where you are?" He said with disbelief. "Should I?" I asked. He did something totally unexpected, he started laughing. "What? What's so funny?" "Wait til' ya see, kid." He wiped the tears streaming from his eyes, and said, "Follow me", turning towards the door. "No" I said. That one syllable bouncing off the walls of the room. He stopped and looked back, straight into my eyes. "If you want to live, you'll do as I say."

I chuckled, "I can take care of myself just fine, thank you very much." I pushed pass him, heading towards the door. I felt a tingling sensation, the type I usually get before danger strikes. There was a glint of metal just out of the corner of my eye. If it weren't for my instinct, I would have been skewered right there and then. I leapt up straight in the air, just as a shruiken passed under me, the place where my head would have been a few seconds ago. I landed light on my feet, and whirled around to face Griffin. I found him staring open-mouthed at me, a shruiken in his left hand. "What?" I asked, suppressing a grin. "You didn't think I was some kind of average everyday kid, now, did you?" I turned around and exited the room,

17

finding myself in a dimly lit corridor. Griffin hurried behind me, "Who are you?" He asked, finally a bit of respect in his tone. "Firo. The name's Firo Raiden." "Sorry I tried to kill you. I thought you were another stowaway." He said. "Wait, we're on a ship?" I asked, flabbergasted, he just nodded grimly. "We're headed towards the Bermuda triangle." Just then, there was a flashing red light, and alarms started blaring. The noise was deafening in the cramped corridor. "We need to find the weapons room!" I shouted over the noise. He nodded. I felt that I had forgotten something. "SHIT!" I shouted. Night-Eyes! I had absolutely forgotten about her! <Night-Eyes!> I yelled using my mind. <About time you remembered me, Firo.> I felt something moving somewhere behind me. I turned around and saw a shadow emerge from behind the crate. "Night-Eyes" I yelled with delight.

"Stay back kid!" Griffin shouted. "I'll take care of her!" I jumped between them. "NO!" I shouted. He looked confused. "She's my companion." "A jaguar?" he asked. <Yes.> Night-Eyes answered directly to Griffin. He looked startled. "I - I didn't mean to cause offence, miss." <It's okay.>"We need to get to the weapons room!" I said. "But why?" Griffin yelled back. "I need my katana, goddammit!" "A 14 year old boy with a jaguar who knows how to use a katana. Now I've seen everything." He mumbled under his breath. I ignored him, and pressed forward down the narrow corridor. I passed a door that read 'supplies'. There must be something there I could use, I thought, something besides a mop.

I opened the door, finding myself in a broom closet. Well, on the bright side, it was a big broom closet. "What are you doing?" Griffin demanded. I held up my hand for silence, and he obliged. I looked a r o u n d f o r a w h i l e, a n d s a w a l e v e r. Why not? I mused.

I pulled the lever, and to my surprise, the wall rotated. It was a dummy wall! <Be careful Firo.><Yeah, I will.> I stepped into the darkness, and found myself in a brightly lit room. Squinting my eyes, I saw a scientist with his back turned towards me.

What? Again? They were probably mass producing them in the hundreds! I approached him stealthily, and snapped his neck, killing him instantly. I heard Griffin and Night-Eyes behind me. I looked around, and gasped when I saw the wall in front of me. "Oh yeah," I said with a grin, "That'll do just fine." I saw Griffin smirking, and I felt Night-Eyes' excitement. I equipped myself, and headed towards another door at the other end. I barged out, and found myself on the upper deck. I stood shocked, my mind reeling. All around me, blue! I really thought for a moment that the world was taken over by a huge smurf army! I really was on a ship. I could hear the alarms, still blaring, down below. "Come on!" I pestered. I started towards the life rafts, when, there was a scream behind me. I turned around, and saw Griffin holding the neck of a dead white-coat. I just shrugged, and continued walking. There were crates and boxes lying everywhere. I stopped, hearing voices right around the corner. I pulled out my SPAS- 12 shotgun, ready for action. Yeah, that's right. A friggin' shotgun! I ducked behind a container, out of sight. I signaled to Night-Eyes and Griffin to follow suit. They dived behind a crate, just before a patrol came into view.

I held my breath, hoping they'd just go away. One of the guards came closer to the crate. I tried my best to look inconspicuous… well, as inconspicuous as a 14 year old with a shotgun can look. It was just my luck that he didn't bother looking. I could have taken care of him before he could say 'My knickers are ablaze!' I signaled to Griffin and Night-Eyes to keep it down. I peeped over just to see the patrol go back around the corner. I stood up, looking for any means to escape. Griffin came behind me. "I think I might know a way off this ship. I saw an auto garage down below deck, there might have been a few jet skis. We could use them to bust the heck outta here. He exclaimed. "I think you've overlooked something, Griff." I said. "What?" He had a confused look on his face. "If we go down, we'll go down with style, baby!" he grinned at me. Night-Eyes, too, looked pleased. For the first time in weeks, I finally had a plan! I set off towards the lower decks with newfound determination with Griffin and Night- Eyes following. I found a doorway set between 2 fire extinguishers. "Think this might be it?" I asked. Griffin nodded affirmatively.

I pushed open the door, and found a set of stairs leading down below. It was pitch black, so I groped around the walls for a bit, hoping to find a torch or a lamp. And frankly, I fight better in the light. I found a torch after a few minutes of groping around.

"Here, use this." I tossed one to him. I turned mine on, the light blinded me for a few seconds, but I adjusted to it quick enough. <Stay close> I said to Night-Eyes. I descended the stairs, mind on overdrive. I arrived at the bottom of the stairs, to find myself in another room. This one well lit. It was empty, except for a single white panel in the dead center. The screen was flashing blue. I stepped forward wondering what the heck it was. I just had taken a step forward, when Griffin squealed with delight. I turned back, and saw that he had just arrived. <Ask him what the flashing-blue-screen is.> Night-Eyes said. "Do you know what it is?" I asked. "Hell yes!" he replied with a flourish. "Well? What is it?" "It's a weapons panel!" "I don't mean to rain on your parade, but I don't see any weapons here. And plus, we already have weapons." "I know. But would you prefer a rusty old shotgun? Or a machine gun?" "M a c h i n e - g u n, o f c o u r s e ! "I s n o r t e d . Well then, that's why there's a panel over here."

That shut me up. I took to exploring the walls, Night-Eyes by my side. It was a different material from the rest of the ship, as far as I could tell. "Yo, Griff, what are these walls made up of?" "Graphene" "What's that?" I asked. "It's like steel, only 200 times stronger. You're going to need much more than a hand grenade to blow this place up. It's more or less a nuclear bunker." Night-eyes felt uneasy, <Firo, where are we going to?>"Griffin said something about a triangle; I don't know what it meant, though." Just then, there was a metallic beeping noise, and Griff gave a shout of excitement. There was a whirring noise, and a doorway a p p e a r e d, s e e m i n g l y o u t o f n o w h e r e. "Well, it's now or never." Said Griffin. I led the way through the doorway. It was big enough for the three of us to walk side by side. The dimly lit corridor looked measly compared to the previous room.

We walked cautiously, straining our ears to catch the slightest sounds. There was another door at the end. This one looked as formidable as a dead opossum. Griffin kicked the door open, the wood exploding into fragments.

"Doesn't seem like anyone's been using this room, right?" I asked. "Don't be fooled by looks, Firo. They disguise everything over here. Why, just last week, I had to use the restroom so bad, and after a long search for one, I stumbled into a toilet disguised as a broom-closet and did my thing. I think it was a broom-closet, though." He said. We entered the room; Night-eyes immediately started sniffing around. Griffin took to checking a dusty old bookshelf at the far end. I saw something glint on the ceiling. I thought it was peculiar, but I dismissed it. I stepped past the cobwebs, and found myself in what seemed to be the kitchen. My rumbling stomach reminded me of my hunger. I spotted a fridge, and found it filled with goodies! Cookies, butterfingers, toffees, sandwiches, cokes, you name it and it was probably here. I wolfed down on whatever I could, and the rest went into my pockets. I found a backpack on a table, and hefted it onto my back. Within seconds, the entire fridge was empty. I headed back the way I came from, I saw Griffin and Night-eyes rummaging through some drawers. Griffin was saying something to Night-eyes, I couldn't shrug off the feeling that they were talking about me.

"Guys, I've gotten us some grub!" "Mmm, I'm starving!" Griffin exclaimed, and proceeded to shovel sandwiches down his throat, not stopping even to chew. Night-eyes had a few jawbreakers; she was addicted with them the moment she tasted a particularly big one.

<ILOVETHEM!>she shouted. "Okay, okay! Just keep it down!" I said. While they were munching, I took the liberty of continuing where they left off. I saw that Griffin hadn't checked his drawer quite proper. There seemed to be a hollow compartment below the last drawer. After a bit of scratching and splinters, I took the false bottom off. What I saw wasn't of much interest, an alcohol bottle; Jack Daniels, an empty cigarette box; Dunhill, a pair of reading glasses, and a key. I took out the key. It looked like any ordinary key, except for the engravings. It was covered with them, in some other language. After much closer examining, I realized that it was made of the same material I saw back in the 'Weapons panel' room. "Hey Griffin, I never did see any weapons. What was that panel supposed to do, anyways?" I shouted to him.

"I guess the walls were supposed to rotate, but sometimes if there's a jam, there'd be a plan B. something like what's happening now. There's supposed to be some sort of key, or a card that'd open another panel. A back-up panel, if you will." "Well then Griffin, looks like our lucky day." I showed him the key I found. He looked confused for a bit, then his face changed from shock, to surprise, and finally to relief. He took it from me, looking at it intently, probably for some more clues. Night-eyes nudged me gently, <Firo, I heard something outside. We'd better finish off soon.> No sooner than she said it, there was a crash and a shout right out the door. Griffin, Me and Night-eyes stood alert, hoping desperately that it was an animal or something else, besides a human. There were some more footsteps outside, it was then when I remembered the glint in the ceiling. I looked up, and there it was! I shuffled closer, pushing past Griffin, trying to get a better look.

Suddenly, there was a loud BANG! I felt something whizz past my ear, missing it by a fraction of an inch. "I found them!" Someone shouted. Griffin took charge at once, shouting at us to duck behind the couch.

No sooner than we'd done that, there was a hail of bullets passing through where we stood a second earlier. "You think we got 'em?" I heard someone ask. "Definite. No one could've survived that!" 'Well fellas, I'm sorry to disappoint ya'll, but I'm alive!' I thought. Griffin motioned for me to shut up. Night-eyes had her ears pricked. There were some more voices outside; I guessed that there were about 20 of them. "We need to get out of here, fast! We can't take on all of them in a fight; we'll get pulverized!" I whispered urgently to Griffin. There was some murmuring, followed by some shuffling footsteps. I peeped over the couch to find everyone standing at attention, facing away from our spot. Quite surprisingly, my prediction was scarily accurate, there were 23 men. I pulled up Griffin next to me, wanting him to see what the heck was happening. There was a little trumpet blown, and all of the men saluted. Some sort of Officer, I suppose, walked through the door. I couldn't see his face that clearly, but I was sure I know him. It sounded stupid when I said that to Griffin, but he looked serious when He listened.

The Commander asked a few questions, and if my ears worked proper, I could've sworn that he said something about ninjas on the ship. It took me by surprise, Ninjas? On a ship? That did sound pretty weird. But a wave of relief crashed over me. They weren't looking for us! They were on the hunt for Ninjas! I crept out from behind the couch after everyone had gone. I walked over to Griffin, who looked pale as a ghost. "What's wrong?" I asked with alarm. "There're ninjas on this ship." He whispered. I nodded. "I overheard them talking about capturing them, so we don't have anything to worry about"

<I think someone's in the next room, Firo. > Night-eyes thought spoke with me. <Is it something to be worried about?> I asked. Night-eyes just looked at me grimly. I gulped, and motioned for Griffin to follow us. I slowly stepped out of our room, and followed Night-eyes, unsure of what I might face. I walked on, unaware that Night-eyes had stopped. <Firo!>the urgency in her voice made me stop right where I stood. <Firo, there's a patrol coming around the corner, Hide!> I immediately ducked into an empty room, or so I thought. I closed the door, leaning on it with my back. The room was pitch black, I felt around for a switch.

I found one, and flipped it on.

There was a rumbling sound, and the clanking of some chains. But that was it. I felt around some more, and found another switch. Hoping that this was the one, I flipped it. There was a flash, and the room was bathed in fluorescent light. What I saw made me gag on my own bile. The room was had no furniture whatsoever except for 4 chairs. These weren't ordinary chairs; they were electric, most probably. And judging from the smoke emitting from one of the panels, it had already been used. But that wasn't the bad part. There were PEOPLE on the chairs! I hurried to the first person, the sight made me puke all over the side of his chair. The body was charred black, like an over-burnt piece of toast. The person, it seemed to me that it was a man, lay still. The stillness you only get from a dead body. I pulled my face away from the gruesome scene. I noticed that the other three panels seemed to be untouched. I moved towards the second chair. I gasped in shock, it was Scotty! I felt the weight of guilt lift off my shoulders. I saw that Mark and Scar were here too! I hurriedly thought spoke with Night-eyes. <Get in the room fast, Night-eyes! Bring Griffin with you.>

Not a second later, the door barged open, and Night-eyes jumped in with a growl, her shackles raised.

<Where are they?> Griffin stepped behind her, looking menacing as well. "It's okay! There's nothing to worry about!" I shouted, excited by my find. "Look who I stumbled upon!" Night-eyes looked at what I was pointing at, and gave a yelp of surprise. <We found them! We found them!> She shouted in glee. "Griffin, help me with these" I pointed at the panels. "I think they control the release mechanism." He walked over to Marks' panel, and set to work, Night-eyes by his side. <I'll be over here> I said to Night-eyes. Wandering through the room, I realized that this was some sort of torture chamber!

I saw a mini guillotine, an iron maiden and a whole lot of others that looked severe. There was a rotting stench emitting from a corner, and after some close investigation (And some more puke), I realized that someone had dumped all of their victims over here. I reeled myself away, heading back towards Night- eyes and Griffin, when I noticed something shine on one of the walls. I thought I had seen that somewhere before, when it hit me! It was in the abandoned room! I quickly checked my pockets, looking for the key. I fished it out, and pushed it into the lock.

A perfect fit! I turned the key in the lock, wondering what would happen. There was a creaking sound, and a little squeak, but that was all.

I felt a little disappointed, then without warning, there was the unmistakable sound of gears whirring, and a door I hadn't noticed opened, quietly. Excited by my find, I hurried to Griffin. He had just finished working on the second panel by the time I came back. I looked at the first chair, and saw that Mark had been released of his bonds, and now lay unconscious. Night-eyes was sniffing at something behind Griffin. Whatever I was about to say slipped my mind, because I heard voices out in the hallway. "Griffin!" I hissed. "We might have company!"

He turned around, nodding at me. Just then, there was a groan from Scar. I saw that all the three of them were free. <Night-eyes, do you have any clue of how many people might be there outside?>

<Just a moment, Firo> She crept up to the door, eased it open just a teeny bit, and peeped outside. She turned around with fear in her eyes. <There are over fifty of them! We can't fight them!>

"No worries," I said, "I found a secret passageway over there at the back." Griffin looked at me funny, and asked "How did you find it?"

"Remember the key? Turns out it has a lot more use than I thought it would!" I hefted up Scar, Griffin with Mark. I found a bit of rope on a table, and secured it to Scotty. <Night-eyes, you pull Scott. He's not that heavy, so it'll be easy> I heard the sound of grunting behind the door, and I figured that they had found us. It was just a matter of time before they broke through the door.

I led the way to the passageway, and I was greeted by a shout of surprise. No doubt Griffin. But no time to think.

I herded all of them into the narrow stairway, waiting until all of them were in. I went in the last, just as the first hinges of the door gave way with a loud *CRACK!* I panicked for a moment when the door didn't close behind me, but there was a shudder, and suddenly, I was enclosed in darkness. I felt my way through the pitch-black tunnel, feeling every step for booby-traps. Its times like these when you'd really appreciate some of those irritating flashing neon signs.

I finally found myself in an enormous cavern. At least that's what I think it was, judging by the sound of my echoes. That was surprising, but just then I bumped into Griffin. "What's wrong?" I asked.

"Shut up!" He hissed. I was confused for a while, when it dawned on me. There was a deep throaty gurgle every ten seconds. Night-eyes stood, shackles raised, teeth bared ready for action. <Night-eyes! What is that thing?!> <I'm not sure, Firo. But let's hope it doesn't know we're here> Night-eyes suddenly yelped, and dashed away. I didn't know what was wrong, until I saw the giant clawed hand come down upon me. I dived for cover, hoping Griffin and Night-eyes along with Mark, Scar and Scotty. I scratched myself pretty bad on the rough sand. But I'd choose a little cut, rather than become the appetizer for some giant beast whose name I didn't know!

There was a deafening screech; I felt blood running down the side of my cheek. "Griffin! Night-eyes!

Where are you?"

I shouted at the top of my lungs. "We're okay!" Came a shout from somewhere to my left. I turned b l i n d l y, u n a b l e t o j u d g e my d i r e c t i o n . I prayed and prayed that the beast wouldn't smash me to a pulp. I hefted myself off my knees, and stood up a little wobbly.

I heard the sound of machine gun fire; it lighted up the cavern for a millisecond. But in that millisecond, I almost crapped my pants. I caught a glimpse of the monster, something that brought out all the fears that I had. Its face certainly did NOT look like one.

There wasn't a nose, just 5 slits below its jaw. It had eyes, alright. But they were on its chest! Not to mention that they were a purple color! The mouth was where the eyes usually are. But the scary part? The head was constantly changing shape, like an amoeba. And not any ordinary shape, it transformed into your deepest fears, taking control of your mind, paralyzing it. I stood there transfixed, even after darkness enveloped me. I slapped myself mentally, pulling out my gun. I had absolutely no idea where to shoot, of course. Just then, thankfully, there was another burst of machine gun fire. I spotted the creature. I bounded towards it, taking aim as I did. I shot from about 4 meters away. I was definitely not prepared for the immense recoil! I landed on my butt, just as the creature gave a wail. I looked closer, squinting my eyes. I saw that my aim was true! One of its eyes was a gooey mess, purple liquid flowing out like the Niagara Falls. <Night-eyes! Where are you?> I yelled mentally in all directions.

<It's okay Firo, I'm fine. I've got Mark, Scar and Scott with me. It's Griffin who needs help. Go!> There was an Almighty rumble that came from the ceiling. I was distracted for a minute, and then Griffin came barreling out of nowhere, crashing into my chest. I lost my balance, and fell to the ground, hitting my elbow pretty hard. Griffin let out a moan of pain. "My ankle." He whimpered. It was then I realized what had happened. There was a reason that room was left unguarded. It was on purpose. We were intended to be used as BAIT.

The creature loomed above me, staring right into my eyes. I looked away, avoiding its gaze, when all of a sudden; Night-eyes pounced onto the beast. <Night-eyes! Be careful!> I yelled. There wasn't a response, instead, she clawed at the beast's other eye, rendering it blind to the world. "Yeah!" I shouted in triumph. But my excitement was short lived, as the creature yanked her off its face, and lobbed her to the opposite wall. There was another crash, as more and more boulders fell down. The beast roared in defiance, challenging anyone to attack. I looked up at it, and was surprised at what I saw.

Three more black figures were scaling the creature's back. 'That's odd' I mused, just as a sound behind me alerted Griffin, who had now gotten his balance, and stood ready with his gun. I whirled around, only to find a fist flying straight at me. The next thing I knew, I was out cold.

Chapter 3

NINJA

opened my eyes to harsh industrial lighting, and silently panicked. *Where am I? What happened? The last thing I remember was a broken nose.*

I tried standing up, and fell off my table/bed. I pulled myself up, and looked around at my 'room'. What I was sleeping on seemed to be a metal table. I remembered Night-eyes, Griffin and the others. I stood at attention, straining my ears for the slightest noise. I spotted a door, and headed towards it. Pushing it open, I found myself in some kind of meeting room. There was a huge table in the center, and lots of chairs. There was a computer on the table. A matchbook, to be exact. I ran towards it, switching it on. A dialogue box popped up.

Password required for authentication.

"Oh Crap! I forgot about the password!" I typed in a few of my guesses, but obviously, they didn't work. I was figuring out some more words, when someone coughed gently behind me. I turned around, flailing my arms. "Whoa! Stop! Stop it!" I did so, and saw that it was Scotty. "Scottster! I thought you were a goner for sure!"

I playfully hit him backside on his head. "Don't you ever do that again?" I said. He just grinned.

"Listen, there are reports of Ninja on this ship, have you seen any? We need to be careful, you, me, Night-eyes, Mark and Scar." I said. He just looked at me with a mischievous glint in his eyes, something I'd never seen before. I turned around and asked him, "Hey, do you know the password to this computer? Stupid thing won't let me access it."

He nodded, and took control of the laptop. In a few seconds, the all too familiar desktop of the OS opened up.

"Scotty, where are Mark and Scar?"

"Oh don't worry about them; they're in the back room." He said, pointing at a metal door.

"How exactly did you land up on this ship?"

"I thought you'd have a little more faith in me, Firo! I came to rescue you!" He said, with a sly smile.

"Well, it looks like your plan back-fired. I'm the one doing all the saving!"

He laughed. I looked through he files, hoping to find any sort of clue, or even a hint of what was happening.

"You won't find anything in there, Firo." "How do you know that, uh?"

"Well, it's my computer, so…" I put it away, embarrassed.

I headed towards the metal door, wanting to talk to Mark and Scar. I was about to push open the door, when Scotty rushed past me, planting himself between me and the door.

"What's wrong?" I asked, puzzled.

"Oh, nothing. It's just that they're pretty tired, so we should let them rest, you know, relax."

"Oh, okay then." I looked around, I don't see any ladder."

But before he could answer, Griffin came barreling through the metal door, shoving it open like it was a Chinese take-away box.

"Griffin!" I exclaimed. I'd never been so happy to see a person who nearly tried to kill me with a shruiken. I noticed a gash that ran from his left elbow all the way to his wrist.

"What happened?" I asked, concerned. "Oh, nothing to worry about," He said. "It's just a tiny cut. It'll go away in a few weeks."

That was the understatement of the year. That gash looked bigger than my entire arm! "Griffin, what is this place?

You remember about the general? Do you think that he did this to us?"

He just looked at me, then at Scotty, and back at me.

There was something different about his eyes, like they held a terrible secret. "We're not in t-trouble, are we? Do you think that the N-Ninja kidnapped us?" I stammered, finding no other door apart from the room/closet I just came out from.

"Wait, where's the exit?" I asked. He just pointed to a trapdoor set in the ceiling. Finding no ladder, I asked, "How do you guys get up there?" The table's too low for you and I don't see any ladder..."

"Firo, we need to talk."

"Sure. What is it?" I asked.

"You see, I haven't been completely honest with you all this time." He said, looking at Scotty for support.

"With what?" I asked, feeling a little suspicious.

"Remember the time when we first met? And you asked me what I did for a living before I got on the ship?"

"Yeah. So?"

"Well, I'm not a pen salesman. Honestly? I'm…. I'm a Ninja."

"Ha-ha! Good one, Griff," I snickered, "If you're a Ninja, then why not say that I'm a monkey in a tuxedo made out of bacon, holding a light saber, sitting on a robot unicorn racing towards a burning shuttle headed to the Sun."

He just looked at me, dumbfounded for a few seconds, and looked at Scotty. He sighed, and turned to me. "Look, Firo. I know you might not believe anything I might say right now, but you've gotta trust me." He said something to Griffin in…in French? Griff went over to the metal door, and opened it for me. He gestured for me to come, and I did.

What I saw inside almost blew my head away. Literally. There was an arrow notched at me!

As I ventured in deeper, I realized that this was no back-room. It was a weapons lair! And I'm willing to bet that there were enough weapons to supply the entire population of Germany!

I noticed this particularly thick bludgeon that could probably knock King-Kong out. I saw some sort of a showpiece, a display.

And would you guess what was on it? That's right! My katana! My beautiful, beautiful katana!

I ran towards it, almost tripping over a huge bow. I yanked the katana off its stand, holding it close to me. I never knew anyone could be attracted to a weapon so much, but now, my doubts were cleared away.

I walked a little further, and saw weapons that would've made Chuck Norris cry!

I picked up a hand gun that looked like a cross between a light saber, a machine-gun and a sniper. It wasn't very heavy, so I thought I'd keep it.

I stowed it away in my pocket. I turned around and saw that Griffin was doing the same. I decided to look for a shield, I needed one desperately! I walked around for about a half-hour before I found one. And yes, the room was that big. I spotted a wrist- band that looked flashy. It had the Adidas logo on it. I picked it up and put it on. It didn't do much. I was about to turn around when I saw it. Words could not describe how I felt when I laid my eyes on that beautiful piece of weaponry. It was full-body armor.

The entire suit was a crimson red, my favorite color!

I lifted it up, and was surprised by its weight! It was no heavier than my sword. I donned it on, feeling energy course through my body the moment it touched my skin.

I slid out my katana, and gasped at my reflection. It looked like a dragon covered my body! The designs were excruciatingly detailed. I looked like a warlord dressed for battle!

I hadn't found a shield, but with this outfit, who needs one?

I shook my hand, to loosen up the wrist-caps, when there was a click, a small whirr. Without warning, the band tightened over my wrist. Although it didn't hurt me, it sure surprised me! But that wasn't it, the band slowly expanded, and before I knew it, there was a fully formed shield sitting on my arm. It too was a crimson red, not too surprisingly.

Well, what do you know? If you minus the giant monster, and me stuck on this ship, it was my lucky day! I looked down, wanting to compare the design and details with my armor and my wrist-shield.

My body wasn't there! It wasn't like some cheap magic trick, no. It was like I blended in with my surroundings, just like a chameleon!

I hoped that my armor could also be retracted, like my wrist-band.

But I couldn't figure it out. I shook, wiggled, wobbled and even jiggled. I found a bulge on my helm, and pressed it. Instantly, my armor morphed into clothes! Jackpot! I walked over to where Griffin and Night-eyes were. <Night-eyes!> I thought-spoke.

<I'm over here, Firo.>

I walked over to Griffin, and saw him handling a golden shruiken. "Griff, have you been here before?"

"No, it's my first time." He said, sounding a little awestruck.

"Listen, were you serious when you said that you were a Ninja?" I asked, a little skeptical.

He looked at me, picked up a breastplate, threw it in the air and diced it into 8 quarters with two shruiken. "Proof enough?"

"Yeah." I answered, putting on a poker face.

<Firo, let's go. I feel uncomfortable over here.>

<Sure>

I walked back towards the door, leading Griffin and Night-eyes. "Griffin, where are Scar and Mark?"

"Who are they?" He asked confused.

"You don't know them?" "Nope. Not a clue"

I spotted Scotty outside the room, and barreled towards him like a bull. I crashed right into him, throwing him down. I bent over, grabbed him by the collar, and pulled him up to my face. "What the hell have you done with Mark and Scar?" I screamed at his face. "Where are they?" I demanded.

"I d-don't know what you're talking about!" He stuttered.

I smacked him across his face, "Don't make me go all animal over you, you worthless piece of scum!

Where have you hidden Mark and Scar? Answer me!"

Griffin and Night-eyes just stood there transfixed.

<Firo! What are you doing?><Don't worry. Right now I need you to hold him in place.>

She didn't answer; she just came over and lightly clamped her jaws over his right arm.

"Move a muscle, and Night-eyes over here will chew your arm off like a piece of lickerish. Are we clear? Or should I repeat?" I asked him, raising my katana for effect. He whimpered. "Get up!" I barked. He stood, swaying on the spot. I grabbed him by the nose, and pulled for all it was worth. It came off! Well not only the nose, but his entire face. It was a silicone-gel mask!

Underneath the mask was a thin teenage boy, about 17 or 18 years old. His face suggested a truly bad case of acne. It was like the surface of the moon! He had auburn hair, speckled with dandruff. He seemed harmless enough, until he brought out his grenade.

He just pulled it out of his trouser pocket, put it between his teeth, and held the pin with his index finger.

"Wait!" I shouted, "Don't do it!" He just looked at me, and tightened his finger on the pin. At first I thought that we were screwed. But at the last second, Night-eyes jumped onto Mr. Suicid3, making him lose his balance. It was just my luck that the grenade slipped from his teeth. I smacked him across his head with the butt of my Katana. "Griffin. Do you know him?" I asked. "Never seen him in my life. I knew Scotty, but I thought this person was him. I've been played all along, huh?" I knew Griffin well enough to understand that he was telling the truth. I pulled the unconscious body towards the weapons room, when Night-eyes froze. Literally, she froze. There was ice around her. As if she was a Popsicle. I ran over to her hand started hacking at the ice. "Help me!" I shouted over to Griffin. He rushed over and pulled out his golden shruiken. There was a rumble; I turned around, surprised, when Griffin held up his hands to stop me. I was wondering what was happening, just as an almighty crash brought the ceiling down.

It was as unexpected as a chicken reading a book made out of string cheese! I fell down hard, hoping Griffin and Night-eyes probably did the same to escape the hail of rocks. I peeped over the rocks in front of me, and saw something that sent a chill down my spine. Three Ninja stood where the laptop once was.

They looked fierce, their black shinobi outfits made them look like demons in the dim lightning. I caught a glimpse of golden shruiken, exactly like the one Griffin had.

<Night-eyes!> I shouted using thought-speak. <Firo! Over here! I think Griffin sprained his ankle, I'm sure it's not supposed to be turned in that angle.> I spotted them just a few meters away from the Ninja. 'They need a distraction!' I thought. <Night- eyes, on the count of three, I want you and Griffin to run into the weapons room. Okay?>

<What do you have in mind?> I explained my plan to her, and surprisingly, she accepted it. <Tell this to Griff, make sure he's ready. Or else this plan is a complete failure before it even starts.>

I peeped over again, and saw that the Ninja were whispering in Japanese. <Okay. One. Two. Aaand Three! GoGoGoGoGo!> I screamed my head off. I jumped over the debris, in plain sight of the Ninja. I slid out a spare shruiken and threw it towards them. Unfortunately, it missed. Fortunately? I definitely got their attention. They stood staring at me, for a second I thought that they would return my shruiken with added benefits. But they did something even more surprising. They snickered at me. Well, I suppose I would've done the same if I saw a 14 year old wielding a deadly blade. But guess what? Not every 14 year old is Firo Raiden. I grinned to myself, and beckoned to them to attack.

Time for them to taste the wrath of Firo!

I saw Night-eyes help Griffin hobble over to the room, and close the door behind them. I was relieved that that was over.

One of the Ninja, a little on the plump side, walked boldly towards me, carrying a sword. He chuckled to himself, mumbling something about stupid kids. I gripped the hilt of my blade, ready to slice 'n dice at the smallest hint of aggressiveness. He stood right in front of me, waving his blade in front of my face, taunting me. I whirled my blade around my head, and brought it crashing down onto his sword, disarming him instantly. He stood there, open-mouthed. "Catching flies?" I asked, just before I sliced him into human sized patty in less than a second.

His 'friends' stood in shock too. I waved my Katana at them. Instantly, they slid out their shruiken, and lobbed them at me.

I'd love to say that I deflected them off my blade, and sent them ricocheting back at my attackers, but that's not what happened. I dived for cover, scraping my elbow as I did. The shruiken buried themselves in the wall behind me. They lumbered towards me, this time with their blades out. I knew I was a goner. Just then there was a bang, and my assaulters looked back, distracted.

It was all I needed. I kicked their feet out from under them, and they fell to floor with a loud *THUD!* The door to the weapons room opened, and Griffin hobbled out, looking as harmless as a rat caught in a mousetrap.

What made him look bad-ass was the minigun he was cradling in his arms. Night-eyes walked by his side, looking equally dangerous. "Ok, where are those wieners?" Griffin demanded.

"Its okay, Private Pain. They're taken care of." I said with a smirk. He looked a little disappointed, I could tell.

"Hey, check this out. Remember the golden shruiken you found in the weapons room? They have it too." I p o i n t e d a t t h e b o d i e s o n t h e f l o o r. He went over there, and after close examination, he returned to me, his face deathly pale. "We have to get off this ship now!"

"Why? What's wrong?" I asked.

"These are rogue Ninja. From my clan. I...I haven't exactly been truthful to you this whole time." He said. "It's okay. I'm not going anywhere, and neither is Night-eyes." He looked at me, took a deep breath, and began. "You see, I'm a *wye*. A runaway Ninja, much like these gentlemen over here." He said with a grin. I returned it with a cold hard stare. He gulped nervously, and continued.

"I ran away when I was 17 years old. My parents were traitors to our clan, and we had to escape. But we couldn't run forever, and soon, they found us. My clan isn't much of a human rights' follower. They murdered my father, and gave me a knife, telling me that they would burn me over an open spit if I didn't kill my mother." He said.

I didn't know how to respond to that. A tear silently rolled down his cheek, onto his lips. I could almost relate to that, except I didn't kill my mother, or my father. "This shruiken, the golden ones, were considered to be the greatest honor if you owned one. My father had three of them, my mother had four. We were one of the most respected family in my clan, so you could imagine their anger. We were considered as traitors, branded as criminals. Why? Because of one single piece of weaponry!" He spat in disgust. "Everyone thought we were fierce warriors. But when my mother, the town's seamstress, found those four golden shruiken, everyone thought that she had stolen them, that we had conspired to steal them. We were chased out of our own house for crying out loud!" He shouted. Just then, there was a low rumble, and an alarm started beeping.

There was a label underneath the alarm that read –*PRESSURIZED CONTAINMENT ALARM*

"Griffin, what the hell does that mean?" I asked.

"There's a water leak, probably in the lower decks…The ships going down!" He said, alarmed.

I dashed towards the weapons room, and desperately began searching for a life vest, or any other object that would keep me alive.

"It's no use, Firo. They've got nothing. I've looked for stuff before, and trust me, I've looked everywhere."

I breathed a sigh, and turned around. "Ok, Griffin, what do you suggest that we do?" I asked, a little annoyed.

He walked over to the storage room, and disappeared into it for a moment. I followed him inside, and saw him hunched over a sink. "Griffin, the ship is sinking, and you're worried about personal hygiene?"

"Oh, shut it." He said. I peeped over his shoulder, and saw him fiddling with the tap. After a few minutes, he shouted "EUREKA!"

"What happened?"

"I remember Scotty, the fake Scotty, telling me about a secret passage-way hidden in this storage- room. This might be it." He said, a little too enthusiastically for a person stuck on a sinking ship.

"It should open rrriiigghhtt about……NOW!"

He turned the knob, and the closet, a small one, rotated into the wall, giving way to a secret passage way. 'Man, this ship would have been paradise for gophers!' I thought, just before entering the dark passage.

Griffin kept behind me, Night-eyes behind him.

We walked for almost an eternity, when we saw the end of the tunnel. I was sweating through my clothes, partly because of the heat, and partly because of what new obstacle I might encounter at the opening.

I walked out onto the deck, the cool breeze drying my clothes and making me feel like an angel, my hair ruffling in the wind. Griffin was right behind me, and Night-eyes behind him, <Firo, are we on the upper- decks?><Hell yeah we are! It's time to get off this goddamn ship!> I walked over to the railing, and surveyed the deep blue ocean. "Griffin, come on over!" I yelled, excited.

He stood beside me, observing our surroundings. Night-eyes stood by my side. I felt like I could take on anything on earth with my friends.

"YAAAA!" I shouted, not caring if anyone heard me. Suddenly, Griffin gave a loud yell. "What happened?" I asked. "LOOK!" He pointed at the horizon. I squinted my eyes, and I saw the distinct shape of an Island. "We're finally going ashore!"

Just then the ship gave a loud creak, and a wave of water crashed onto the deck. "Griffin! We need a boat!"

"How about something even better?" He asked.

"Anything that will help you, me and Night-eyes float." I replied.

He motioned for me to follow him. He led us into a dark room, just opposite to where we were standing a minute ago. "Prepare to be amazed." He said, just before turning on the lights. We stood in a vehicle hangar. There were Jet-Skis, boats, wave-boards, even a bunch of paragliding outfits. You name it, this place definitely had it. I called dibs on a blue Jet-Ski, Griffin stood by an orange one, and Night-eyes stood behind me.

<You're going to have to paraglide, Night-eyes. There isn't place for two on this Jet-Ski. I'm going to strap you in one of them, don't be afraid. We're going to get outta here, and then we'll get what we're really after. Okay?>

She nodded her head. I strapped her into one of the parachutes, and secured her onto the back of the Jet-Ski. "Ok Griff, we're good."

He nodded. "Hold on, Firo. There's going to be a flood of water once I open this hangar. You ready?"

I put on my brave face, and gave him a thumbs-up.

He pushed a red button to his side, and a warning alarm echoed throughout the room. The main door opened slowly, and water trickled out the sides. In a few seconds, the trickle became a gush, and the gush became a flood. "Start your engine!" Griffin yelled from across the room. I held Night-eyes close to me, making sure that her parachute wouldn't get wet.

I turned the key, and the engine roared to life. Within a second, the water had carried us out of the ship, and into the unforgiving waters of the Pacific Ocean. We were completely submerged for a minute or two, but we surfaced, and blasted away from the wreck of the ship. Night-eyes had gone airborne, the wind buffeting her parachute. "I've never done this before!" I yelled over the roar of the engine.

"That makes two of us!" He yelled back.

I laughed, never having this much fun in my entire life.

<Firo! This is amazing!> Night-eyes said gleefully.

<I know!> I replied.

"Um…Griffin? What the heck are we supposed to do now?" I yelled across the water. "The island was east, so we go this way." He yelled back.

I looked behind me, vaguely making out the smoke in the distance, surprised that we had covered so much distance in that much time.

My wrists hurt, and my legs were sore from all the standing up. "Griffin! How much further? I shouted.

"I don't know. Might take a few minutes, a few hours, or even a few days." He said.

I groaned, and pulled the throttle as far as it could go.

Soon, night had fallen, and we were left to navigate using the stars. Not like we knew how to, we didn't.

I could feel the steady hum of the Jet-Ski slowly lose its rhythm. "<Firo, I see land!><Where?> I yelled back using thought-speak. <Up ahead, maybe a kilometer away.>

"Griffin! Land ahoy!" I hollered to him, unable to hide my excitement and relief. "Good. Now I know that there is a God." He said, chuckling to himself.

After hours of Jet-Skiing, we finally washed ashore.

I fell down onto the sand, kissing the ground under my feet.

Night-eyes landed gently beside me. She had fallen asleep during our journey. Griffin lay panting on the sand.

I lifted myself up with wobbly hands, and hobbled over to the trees. The island didn't seem to have much. A few palm trees near the shore, and god knows what lay within the island.

I rested my aching body against a tree. Griffin came over to me, Night-eyes slumped over his shoulder. He carefully rested her down onto the sand. He plonked himself down next to me, and fell asleep at once. Sleep was elusive for me, but as tired as I was, it wasn't hard to catch it. Soon, I was resting my head on Griffin's shoulder, waiting whatever dreams I would get.

I slept long and deep, wishing I would never have to wake.

Griffin shook me awake, and suddenly there was blinding pain all over my body. "Don't fidget; it's only because of yesterday's events." He said, shoving something under my nose.

"Drink it, it might smell bad, but it'll do wonders with your body. It sure did it for me."

As for the smell? It was horrid. It smelled like a skunk that had farted all over a dead gerbil, which was left to rot in a trash can.

I took a sip, and it tasted the same. "So much for honesty." I grumbled. I managed to choke down the rest of the 'Drink'

Instantly, I felt energized.

My body felt it could sky-dive from the Himalayas, with nothing but size XXXL underwear!

"Seems like it does do wonders! How did you know this would work?" I asked.

"Well, I didn't. I was thirsty, so I found this fruit that had this stuff in it. I know it smells bad, but it sure does give your muscles a good shove."

"Where's Night-eyes?" I asked, not finding her around.

"Oh, don't worry about that. She's gone hunting."

I shook myself, and wiped away the sand from wherever I could reach. I walked down to the beach, and the salty breeze flew by my face, freshening me up. Seagulls cawed in the distance, and the waves broke across the shore.

Ignoring the fact that I almost died at the hands of a giant monster, got stuck on a ship and experimented on, almost dying again at the hands of another monster, and escaping an exploding ship, this actually seemed to be a great place to live on. I was just standing there, listening to the sounds, when Night-eyes appeared at my side, looking as though she'd seen a ghost. <Night-eyes, what's wrong?>

<We're not alone on this island, Firo.> Just then, there was a loud bang, a shout and the sound of bones crunching. I ran towards our clearing, fearing the worst. I came to a stop when I saw Griffin holding up a dead rabbit, with a bullet in its head that lay at Griffin's feet.

"Jeez! You scared me to death!" I yelled at him.

"Sorry! Sorry!" He said, "I was just making us dinner."

I looked up, and saw that the sun was already setting.

Griffin looked up at me suddenly, 'Don't move!' He mouthed.

I sat rigid on the spot; Night-eyes did the same.

I probably looked as confused as a dog in a pirate costume. Griffin silently pointed to my left, and I caught a glimpse of a figure crouched in the shadows. <Night-eyes, ask Griffin what we're supposed to do.> I thought-spoke.

After a few seconds, Night-eyes spoke. <He's a native, according to Griffin. Just wait until he goes away or until he shows himself to us.>

I looked at Griffin and mouthed, 'are we in danger?'

He shook his head, and I gave a sigh of relief.

There was some more rustling, and I saw a LOT of shadows crouching behind the trees and bushes.

I looked around, hoping to find any weapon I could use. Right now, even poo seemed like a deadly weapon.

I spotted a good fist-sized rock a little away from where we sat. There was some more rustling, and a man stepped into the clearing. I could make out dozens of pairs of eyes staring at us. The man, he seemed like the leader, looked a little surprised to see us, and little more surprised to see Night-eyes.

He made a few hand gestures, presumably asking us who we were.

I shook my head, not completely understanding him.

He called someone over, and said something to him in the native language, I think. "What's your name?" Asked a guy wearing a turban and a skirt made out of grass. His accent was peculiar; I had never heard anything like it. He pronounced 'name' like 'nayume'.

"I'm Firo," I said, pointing at myself, "He's Griffin", I said, pointing at Griffin, "And that's Night-eyes."

He nodded his head, and turned towards the leader, whispering something in his ear. \

"Wait. Where are we?" I asked the 'Translator'.

He looked back at me, and said, "You be in glorious country. You be in Australia!"

Chapter 4

GRIFFIN'S PAST

I almost fainted from shock. I swear I would've run straight to the beach and try to salvage those Jet-Skis, if *she* hadn't appeared right then.

I never knew that there was such a thing as love, until I saw her. It was exactly like those cheap fairytale romance stories. Time stopped still when I saw her, there was a breeze blowing by, her auburn hair was dancing around her neck. She had the prettiest eyes, dark blue, just like the great ocean. Her strawberry pink lips glistened in the sun. I could give you a list of the things that attracted me to her, but sadly, this book is supposed to be a short one.

I boldly stepped up to her, and said, "Hello there, beautiful. I saw you look at me from over here. What say I take you out to diner….. on the beach?" I said, realizing that this was a really bad idea.

Griffin face-palmed and Night-eyes shake her head sadly.

"Why that's very nice of you, you me and who now?"

She said with a smug look on her face.

"You me and…uhh…Griffishrgj!" I blubbered. I slapped myself mentally for making a fool out of myself. Not that it was new or anything.

She turned away from me and said something to the translator, and retreated back into the woods.

"The daughter of Great leader wants to invite you to be our guests!" He said a little too enthusiastically.

"She's the daughter of him?!" I asked, flabbergasted.

"Yes! Daughter of great leader!" He said, and then turned around to talk to the 'Great Leader'.

I walked back to Griffin and told him that we were guests on this island.

"You really like this girl, no?" Asked griffin, after I was finished.

"Nope. Not one bit." I said, putting on a poker face. Griffin just smiled, and walked over to the translator.

I stood beside Night-eyes. She nuzzled my leg, and curled up into a tight ball at my feet. <When we have to go in, wake me up.> she said.

<Yep, no problem.> I said.

We left a few minutes later, following the high pitched whistle of the leader.

I picked up Night-eyes and hauled her gently over my shoulder, not waking her up.

We walked for a few kilometers, no one uttering a word. Griffin walked right next to me, making hand gestures with some person.

We stopped in a dense clearing, and there was another high-pitched whistle, which was returned with several others.

A few trees just disappeared, and where they stood, lay a narrow cobble-stone road.

"Come on!" The translator barked.

After several minutes of walking, we arrived at the village. I was awestruck the moment I lay my eyes on it. Without my knowledge, we seemed to have hiked uphill, because the houses were carved right into the rocks. The central market-place was bustling with activity, people going to and fro, trying to trade their wares for something or the other. We stopped as a crowd of scantily dressed women crossed our path. One of them winked at Griffin, who surprisingly, blushed!

We walked all the way to what seemed to be the main buildings, probably the leader's quarters. The closer we got the more beautiful and intricate the building seemed to get. We were halted at the main doors, and checked for weapons. Silly them! Our guns and my katana were hanging from our backs. Sadly, they were confiscated.

We entered the great hall, and Griffin literally fell down.

The entire ceiling, the walls, and even the tiles were made out of gold. I mean, if you brought a torch and lit it at one end; you could see it at the other! The entire place was probably the size of 1 ½ football fields.

A kind of car came to pick us up from the entrance. "How old is this place?" I asked the translator.

"The golden palace is 7000 years old. Built by our first king, King Whatte Bouie, it stands for the freedom of our secret little settlement, ciua. They say that the palace keeps expanding, unknown to us." He answered.

Night-eyes squirmed a bit, but that was it. Every room we passed held a new surprise. We passed this one room, where a miniature forest was built. Not plants, flowers, ponds and fruit. Emeralds, rubies, sapphires and diamonds. My eyes nearly fell out of their sockets.

Night-eyes had woken up, and fell silent when she saw where we were. I could feel the ground vibrating underneath us. We stopped at the doors to the Lords' Chamber. "This is the holy meeting place of the council members, From King Whatte Bouie to King Ream Hirer.

The doors were opened, and what I saw was just breath-taking. The hall itself was huge. Palm trees bordered the walls, and there was a miniature pond in the middle, complete with a few white swans, and an intricately carved fountain in the center. <Firo, this is just amazing!> Night-eyes exclaimed.

I didn't answer. There wasn't a need to.

The floor was covered in a sort of reflecting tiles that changed color every time someone walked on it. "That is moonstone my friends. It changes color depending on your mood!" He said gleefully.

The ground underneath my feet was a blue color. "Ha! Your color means that you're tensed!" He said.

'Well, now that the MOST important thing is sorted…" I grumbled. We were stopped once again, and checked for ammunition.

The guard who was checking me got a little too frisky, so I pretended to pick my nose, and rubbed it against my leg.

Good News? He left me alone.

Bad News? I got a lot of dirty stares.

I walked over to Griffin, who was in conversation with the translator. "…So, you say that a…ship exploded? Then you got away on Jet-Skis?" "Yes, yes that's right. Me, Firo -" Griffin was about to complete, when I 'Accidentally' bumped into him.

He looked at me, startled for a minute, but my

Ahem Oh so good-looks brought his memory back to him.

"Hey, can we talk?" I asked.

"Sure. What's up?" He asked me cheerfully. "In private." I said.

I led him to a secluded spot underneath the stairs.

"Griffin-"I began, but just then the translator found us.

"COME!" He yelled right into our ears, transferring a hearty amount of spittle onto my face. He grabbed our wrists and pulled us out. "Great Leader is waiting for you!" We were pushed ahead of the crowd waiting at the foot of the podium, a golden one, of course.

Trumpets sounded through the entire hall, and the translator got onto the stage. "Hail the great leader!" He shouted.

"Hail the great leader!" Responded the crowd.

He moved aside, and the Great Leader stepped up to the podium. The crowd went wild, cheering and waving their hands in the air. "Have you ever seen anything like this?"

He nodded his head, "Nope. Never. Better enjoy it while it lasts!"

"SILENCE!" He said. Although he didn't yell, his words hit us like rocks. The confidence in them was just overwhelming.

"As you all know, our great nation of Australia is in civil war. Our brothers and sisters have turned against each other. We have no one to trust but ourselves. Be sure that there is no traitor amongst us! You can trust me, just as I can trust you.

But not to worry, we have the strongest fortifications in all of Sydney! And an even stronger army! I am telling you this, brothers and sisters, because we have amongst us guests!" He said, pointing at us in the end. I could feel eyes drilling holes at the back of my skull, and not so much different at the front.

"Guests in my castle!" he continued. "They will be treated with utmost respect, and anyone to do so against, will be hanged!" He said, shouting out the last bit.

"A little harsh, don't you think?" I asked Griffin. "They probably have their reasons."

He said something about taxes, and pension, and that was it.

The crowd slowly dispersed, and we were called backstage.

"I am King Rafanta, son of King Ream Hirer." He introduced, giving us a little bow.

"I am Firo Raiden, that's Griffin, and that's…," I turned around to look for Night-eyes, but she wasn't there. Probably gone exploring.

"We haven't had guests over for quite some time now, have we Devin? Hmm?" He asked a boy standing behind his throne.

He shook his head, and looked down.

"King Rafanta-"I began, when he interrupted me "Please, call me Rafanta."

"Rafanta, I don't mean to intrude, but where do you get all the gold, diamonds, rubies and the rest of the precious material?" I asked.

"Oh Haha! Finally, someone finally asks me this! Do you see, Devin? This boy has some courage!" He said gleefully. Devin grinned behind the throne.

"Well, Firo. You see, we are not who you think we are. We are a VERY elusive group of people. We, especially me, make sure that no one finds us. We are the most-"Rafanta began, when Griffin, surprisingly, cut him off.

"YOU are nothing but cheap, deceitful, selfish and a cruel man. You deserve nothing more than an oilskin rag. NOTHING!" Griffin yelled and stormed out. I was startled, and quickly apologized. "Sorry my King, I don't know what happened to him. He's not usually like this. Excuse me." I said, and exited the chamber.

I saw Griffin turn around the corner, just as Night- eyes came out the other.

<No time. Catch up with him. I'll tell you later.> I said.

<Okay.> Night-eyes answered.

I ran towards the opposite side, into the room at the far end. I sat there contemplating on what could be the reason, when I saw something that sent a chill down my spine.

There was a window in the room. It looked pretty old, but that wasn't the problem.

The problem was the view it gave. There was a mine down below, WAY down below, but I could just make out who was doing what and where.

There were children down there! Children from the ages of 8, all the way up to 18. The realization hit me like a train.

'This must've been where Griffin grew up.' I thought.

I sat there staring at the mines below, children and adults alike suffering from the strain of hauling heavy loads on their aching backs.

<Firo!> Night-eyes' voice was faint, but I could hear her.

<Firo, come quick! It's Griffin!>

I hurried out of the room, towards Night-eyes. Judging by the faintness of her voice, she could be far away. Or the gold was acting as a barrier.

I ran towards the podium, and saw a crowd of people heading towards one of the exit doors.

I jumped off the podium, getting a few ugly looks.

I rushed towards the head of the crowd, wanting to see what was happening. "Hey! Quit pushing!"

"Sorry!" "Watch it!" "My bad!"

"Get out of the way, punk!" "Oops!"

I managed to squeeze past the majority of the people.

Before I knew it, I was at the head of the crowd.

<Firo!>

I turned, and spotted Night-eyes a few meters away, Griffin right behind her.

I hopped away from the crowd, stamping a few feet and getting a few insults that would've made a sailor cry.

I landed right in front of her.

"Griffin, what the heck happened back there?"

"I'm sorry. It's just, it's been a really long time since I've been here, and it was that man who made me who I am today. I hate him for all that he's done." He said, sniffing.

"Come on, we're guests here, it can't be that bad to live in luxury for once, right?" I asked.

"Yeah, you're right. I guess I acted stupid and childish."

I pulled him away, back towards the King's chambers.

"Now I know that you've been through a lot over here, and I can't say I know how that feels. But you need to man up and apologize to him."

He nodded, sighed, and proceeded back to where he came from. I and Night-eyes followed behind.

I just crossed the podium, when I caught a flash of auburn hair behind the dais. Only one person I've met so far has that kind of hair.

<Night-eyes, you take Griffin to the King's chambers. I'll join you shortly.>

She nodded, and led Griffin away from me, towards the King.

I turned toward the dais, and hurried towards it.

I turned around a corner, moving according to the footsteps, trusting only my ears to guide me.

The sound of the footsteps led me to a dead end. 'This can't be right!' I thought.

I was just about to turn around, when there was a little squeak. I looked around, and a couple of mice run out of a Grill at the bottom of the wall.

I knelt before it, and tried to pry it open.

After a few tugs and pulls, it came off easily. I pulled it harder and harder until the opening was big enough for me to crawl into. I squeezed into the tight space, hoping I wouldn't get stuck. Death in a shaft. How more embarrassing could that possibly get?

I crawled further and further, deep into the shaft, the hideous stench forcing me to cover my nose with my shirt.

I heard a squeak, and a LOT of scurrying. I checked my pockets, finding a lighter. I tried it, but only after the fourth try did it turn on. I wish it didn't.

What lay before me would've made a grown man pee his pants. Hundreds of mice surrounded me. I mean HUNDREDS! I had never seen so many of them before!

I tried to turn around, to exit, but my shoulders were too broad for me to do a 180. I got stuck!

I panicked, flailing my arms desperately, trying to loosen myself, and at the same time keep the mice away. They had already started crawling over my skin, making me itch all over. I felt one in my pants, and I desperately clawed at it. But no use, there were simply too many of them!

Without any sort of warning, they bit! The pain coursed through my body, making it ache like crazy!

I had never felt such pain before!

Before I knew it, I was growing dizzy. My mind had gone numb. <Night-eyes!> I called out feebly, but she probably couldn't hear me. I last thing I could do, was activate my unused armor, hoping that it would be enough protection.

My senses dulled, and before I knew it, I was out cold, stuck in a drainage shaft surrounded by hundreds, maybe even thousands of flesh-eating mice.

TO BE CONTINUED>>>

Printed in the United States
By Bookmasters